FOLLOW THAT BUS

WRITTEN by SUZAN REID

ILLUSTRATED by C.L.A.MACKENZIE

MRS. TARDY'S class planned a field trip. They were going to take a bus and then a ferry across to Bigby Island for a nice picnic. They had talked about going for a long time and they were very excited.

Mrs. Tardy gathered her clipboard, sent everyone for one last trip to the bathroom, and then they were ready. "Off we go," said Mrs. Tardy.

As the students scrambled for a seat in the back of the bus, Mrs. Tardy checked her attendance.

"We're missing someone," said Mrs. Tardy. "Who's missing?"

"Billy's still in the bathroom," said George.

Mrs. Tardy sighed and called to the driver, "One more on the way!" The driver yawned and nodded his head. The parent volunteers smiled and nodded their heads. Mrs. Tardy stepped off the bus and hurried into the school to find Billy.

He was not in the bathroom. He was not in the classroom. He was not in the hallway.

"Have you seen Billy?" she asked the secretary.

"What are you doing here? Billy got on the bus a minute ago."

"Good," smiled Mrs. Tardy. "Now we can get going."

"Going? They've already gone," said the secretary. She pointed out the window. Mrs. Tardy's mouth fell open as she watched the school bus pull away from the curb and bounce down the street.

"Stop!" yelled Mrs. Tardy from the office window, but the bus did not stop.

"I'll have to catch them in my car!" she exclaimed and off she scurried to the parking lot to find her car.

It was a little old and a little rusty, but it started with a "bang!" and a "pop!" and off went Mrs. Tardy after the school bus.

The car putted along, and when Mrs. Tardy came to the top of the hill, she could see the bright yellow school bus in the distance and she smiled. Then the car wheezed and gasped and crawled to a stop.

"Out of gas!" cried Mrs. Tardy as she watched the bus disappear through town.

Just then a man passed by on his bicycle.

"Stop!" hollered Mrs. Tardy, and he did. Very quickly she explained about the rusty car, the bus and her class, and he agreed to let her borrow his bike. It was a little old and a little rickety, but off she went, whizzing down the hill and heading towards town. She took a shortcut through the park, under the bridge and through the food market. The bike sped along, and as Mrs. Tardy reached the corner of Hurl and Second streets she could see the bright yellow school bus in the distance and she smiled. Then the bike went "snap!" and the pedals flew around and around in a mad frenzy.

"A broken chain!" cried Mrs. Tardy as she watched the bus disappear towards the ferry.

Just then a girl passed by on her skateboard.

"Stop!" hollered Mrs. Tardy, and the girl did. Very quickly Mrs. Tardy explained about the rickety bike, her rusty car, the bus and her class, and the girl agreed to look after the rickety bike while Mrs. Tardy borrowed the skateboard. Mrs. Tardy had never been on a skateboard before, but how hard could it be? she thought.

It was a little old and a little wobbly, but off she went.

She didn't mean to take a shortcut through the baseball field or fish market, but she did. Then she ran into a line of laundry and a garden of roses and kept going.

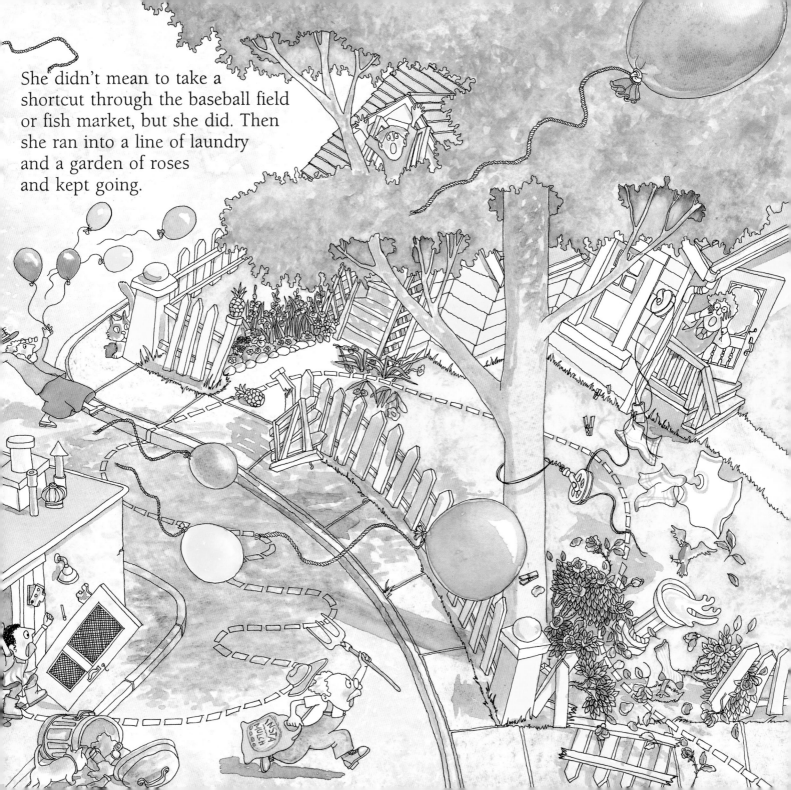

She pulled a sock off her eyes and some rose petals out of her mouth just in time to see the docks, the bus and the ferry, and she smiled. Slowly the ferry began to move away from the docks.

"Stop!" hollered Mrs. Tardy, but it did not stop. Neither did she. Mrs. Tardy and the skateboard flew off the dock and sailed through the air, landing onto the deck of a fishboat.

"Hello," said the man on the boat. Very quickly Mrs. Tardy explained about the wobbly skateboard, the rickety bike, the rusty car, the bus and her class, and he agreed to take her over to Bigby Island. His boat was a little old and a little creaky, but at least they were headed in the right direction.

Mrs. Tardy saw the bright yellow school bus on the ferry and she smiled. Then she noticed that they were moving very slowly.

"Doesn't this thing go any faster?" she cried.

The man frowned and thought for a minute. "Nope," he answered. Mrs. Tardy settled onto the deck and watched the ferry glide through the water in the distance and move farther and farther away.

It took quite a while, but finally they docked on Bigby Island. Mrs. Tardy thanked the man and asked him to look after the wobbly skateboard.

Mrs. Tardy scanned the shore but could see no sign of her class, so she started walking through the sand.

She walked for a very long time and finally, in the distance, she could see a group of people having a nice picnic on the beach. Mrs. Tardy smiled and then she began to run. She ran through the sand and hopped over the logs towards her class. Just as she was getting close to the group, she could see them filing back onto the bright yellow school bus.

"Stop!" panted Mrs. Tardy as she pulled herself over the rocks, but it did not stop.

"Do you need some help?" yelled a woman on a motor boat passing by. "Do you want to get back to the mainland?" Mrs. Tardy nodded. "Swim out and climb aboard then!" Mrs. Tardy waded through the seaweed and paddled out to the boat. She sputtered something about a creaky fishing boat, a wobbly skateboard, a rickety bike, a rusty car, a bus and her class. "Bus. Ferry. Back," Mrs. Tardy gasped as she crawled aboard.

The boat was a little old and a little leaky, but off they went. Mrs. Tardy could see the ferry and the bright yellow school bus just ahead and she managed a weak smile.

The bus rattled off the ferry just as the motor boat reached the docks. Mrs. Tardy thanked the woman, climbed off the boat and looked for a ride back to school.

A garbage truck was loading at the docks. She hobbled over to the drivers and babbled something about a leaky motor boat, a creaky fishing boat, a wobbly skateboard, a rickety bike, a rusty car, a bus and her class. There was no room in the front of the truck, but the drivers offered to take her to the school if she didn't mind riding in the back. It was a little squishy and a little messy, but Mrs. Tardy crawled in.

"Follow that bus," she sighed, and they did, all the way back to school.

The bus pulled to a stop right in front of the school and the garbage truck pulled in behind it. Mrs. Tardy fell out just as the school bell rang.

Happy faces raced off the bus and ran past Mrs. Tardy as she clung to the school fence.

"Bye, Mrs. Tardy!"

"See you tomorrow!"

The parent volunteers staggered off.

"Thanks," one of them said.

"You look tired," another one said.

"I don't think I can make your next field trip," said another.

Mrs. Tardy smiled a silly smile and waved good-bye.

"Ah, you're back," said the principal. "Did you have a good time?"

"Bus. Ferry. Back," blurted Mrs. Tardy.

"Yes," said the principal, "we're very glad you're back too. See you tomorrow."

Mrs. Tardy rested comfortably at home that evening and counted the days until summer vacation.

To David and Kristen, two of my most loyal readers, and
to my friends at Conrad School.
S.R.

To Lillian Sullivan MacKenzie, a true friend and anchor
through the bilge water of life. This really would not have
been done without you. And to Tim for (among other
things) the tunes. And to Ann Featherstone, an editor of
great vision.
C.M.

Text copyright © 1993 Suzan Reid
Illustration copyright © 1993 C.L.A. MacKenzie

Publication assistance provided by The Canada Council.
All rights reserved.

Orca Book Publishers Ltd.
P.O. Box 5626, Station B
Victoria, BC Canada
V8R 6S4

Orca Book Publishers Ltd.
P.O. Box 468
Custer, WA USA
98240-0468

Design by C.L.A. MacKenzie
Printed and bound in Hong Kong

Canadian Cataloguing in Publication Data
Reid, Suzan, 1963-
Follow that bus!

ISBN 0-920501-88-5

I. MacKenzie. Catharine, 1952-   II. Title
PS8585.E44F6 1993   jC813'.54   C93-091077-X
PZ7.R44Fo 1993

10 9 8 7 6 5 4 3 2